Madeline Finn
and the
Library Dog

For all my furry friends and those who love them, thank you.
And for libraries, where the real magic happens.

—L. P.

Published by
PEACHTREE PUBLISHERS
1700 Chattahoochee Avenue
Atlanta, Georgia 30318-2112
www.peachtree-online.com

Edited by Kathy Landwehr
Design and composition by Nicola Simmonds Carmack
The illustrations were rendered in pencil, watercolor, and digital coloring.
Printed in March 2016 by Tien wah Press, Malaysia
10 9 8 7 6 5 4 3 2 1
First Edition

ISBN 978-1-56145-910-0

Cataloging-in-Publication Data is available from the Library of Congress.

Madeline Finn
and the
Library Dog

Lisa Papp

PEACHTREE
ATLANTA

I do NOT like to read!

Not books.

Not magazines.

Not even the menu on the

ice cream truck.

And I ESPECIALLY do not like to read out loud.

"Keep trying, Madeline Finn," my teacher says.

But sometimes I can't figure out the words.

Sometimes the sentences get stuck in my mouth like peanut butter.

Sometimes people giggle when I make a mistake.

And I never get a star sticker from my teacher.

Not even a smiley face.

Instead, I get a heart that says Keep Trying.

I get a lot of Keep Trying stickers.

But I want the star.

Stars are for good readers.

Stars are for understanding words,

and for saying them out loud.

But I know what else they're for.

Stars are for making wishes!

So I make a wish for my very own star.

I guess wishes take a while, because I don't get my star

on Monday or Tuesday.

"Keep trying," my teacher tells me on Wednesday.

On Thursday, I say the frog's name wrong. It's Samuel.

I try to get away with Sam, but it doesn't work.

Friday is no better.

On Saturday, Mom takes me to the library.

"Hello, Madeline Finn," Mrs. Dimple says.

She's our librarian.

"I don't like to read," I remind her, in case she forgot.

"Oh, I remember," she says. "But today we have something special—something you might enjoy."

"Madeline Finn, would you like to read to a dog?"

Mrs. Dimple leads me over to a big white dog.

"This is Bonnie. Why don't you pick out a book to

read to her? She's a great listener."

Bonnie is beautiful. Like a big, snowy polar bear.

"Would you like to try?" Mom asks.

"Yes please," I say. (But not very loud.)

At first, I'm nervous.

I get the letters mixed up.

The words don't sound right.

But then I look at Bonnie, and she looks right
into my eyes. She doesn't giggle.

I feel better. I try again.

Halfway through, I get stuck on another word.

Bonnie doesn't mind. She puts her big paws in
my lap and lets me pet her until I figure it out.

After that, Bonnie and I read
together every Saturday.

It's fun to read when you're not afraid of making mistakes. Bonnie teaches me that it's okay to go slow, and to keep trying—just like the sticker says.

I still don't have a star.

But I can be patient.

Like Bonnie.

Soon, it's almost time to read in class again. But when I go to the library, Bonnie's not there! Neither is Mrs. Dimple.

"Would you like to wait for another dog?" the other librarian asks.

"No thank you," I say, as politely as I can.

"Don't worry," Mom tells me later.

"Bonnie was just busy today."

"But what about school?" I ask.

"You'll do fine," she says. "Just pretend

you're reading to Bonnie."

On Monday morning, I am very nervous.

"Madeline Finn, would you like to read next?" the teacher asks.

"Yes, please," I say. (But still not very loud.)

The first sentence goes pretty well. Then I mess up on a word.
And then another. I hear someone giggle.

But then I think about Bonnie. I take a deep breath and
pretend she's right next to me.

Next thing I know, I'm at the
bottom of the page.

I look at my teacher and she
has a big smile on her face.

I did it! I got my star!

On Saturday, we go to the library again. Mrs. Dimple is back!

"I got my star!" I tell her. "I want to give it to Bonnie."

"Well done, Madeline Finn!" she says.

"I think Bonnie might have a surprise

for you too."

"Madeline Finn, would you like to read to Bonnie—and her puppies?"

"Yes, please!" I say, nice and loud.